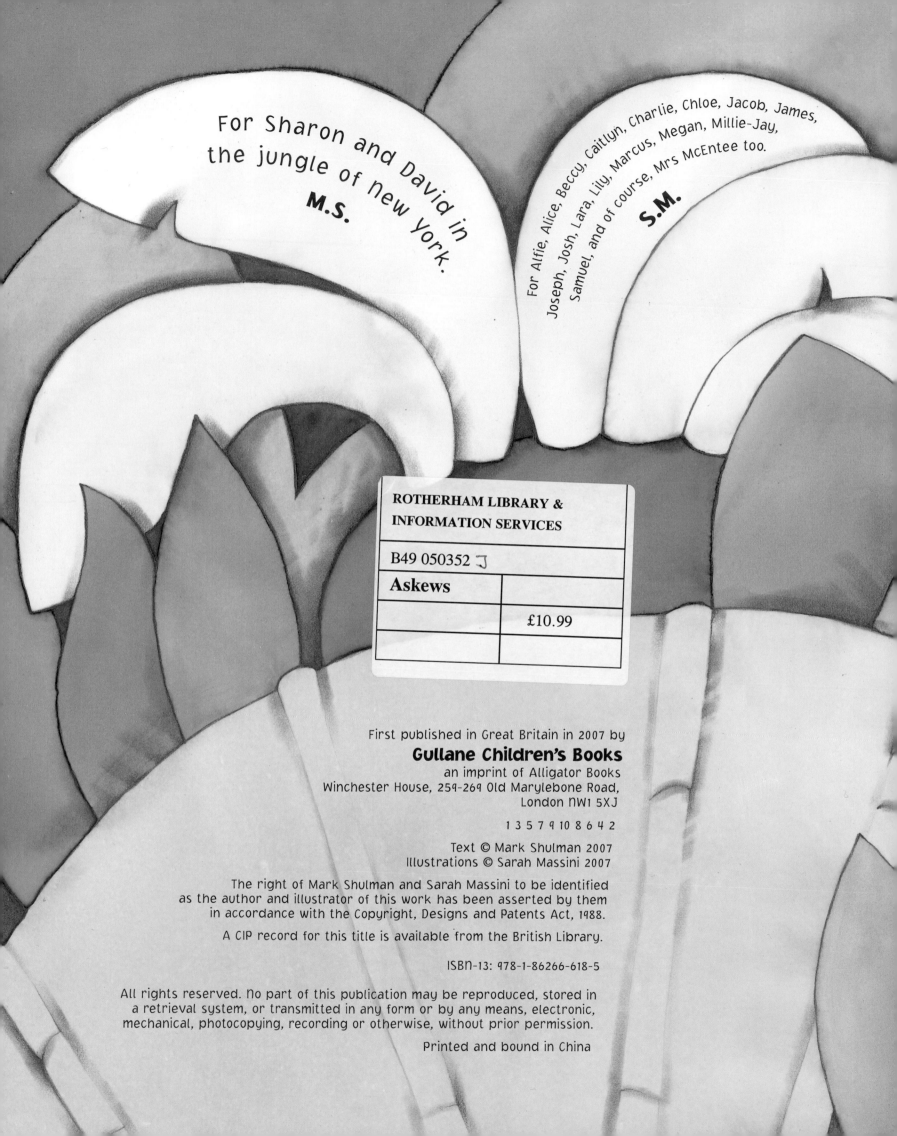

For Sharon and David in the jungle of new York.
M.S.

For Alfie, Alice, Beccy, Caitlyn, Charlie, Chloe, Jacob, James, Joseph, Josh, Lara, Lily, Marcus, Megan, Millie-Jay, Samuel, and of course, Mrs McEntee too.
S.M.

First published in Great Britain in 2007 by
Gullane Children's Books
an imprint of Alligator Books
Winchester House, 259-269 Old Marylebone Road,
London nW1 5XJ

1 3 5 7 9 10 8 6 4 2

Text © Mark Shulman 2007
Illustrations © Sarah Massini 2007

The right of Mark Shulman and Sarah Massini to be identified
as the author and illustrator of this work has been asserted by them
in accordance with the Copyright, Designs and Patents Act, 1988.

A CIP record for this title is available from the British Library.

ISBN-13: 978-1-86266-618-5

Printed and bound in China

Dino in the Jungle!

Mark Shulman

illustrated by Sarah Massini

GULLANE
CHILDREN'S BOOKS

One day, Monkey was swinging all across the jungle.
Suddenly, he stopped. Something tremendous was
coming his way. He heard the leaves crunching.
He saw the mango trees shake.

"It's a . . .

Dinosaur!"

cried the monkey.

"There's a **Dino** in the jungle!"

And he ran so fast he skittered

straight into the parrot's tree.

"Monkey, you should know better. There aren't
any dinosaurs in the jungle," said Parrot.
"So you say!" yelled Monkey.
"But listen . . . listen!"

Then that parrot heard
the leaves crunching.
He saw the mango
trees shake.

"It's a . . .

Dinosaur!

yelled Parrot and Monkey.
"There's a **Dino** in the jungle! Run away!"

And they skittered
right into the
giraffe's meadow.

"You two should know better," said Giraffe.
"There aren't any dinosaurs in the jungle!"
"So you say!" shouted Parrot.
"But listen . . . listen!"

Then that giraffe heard
the leaves crunching. He
saw the mango trees shake.

"It's a . . .

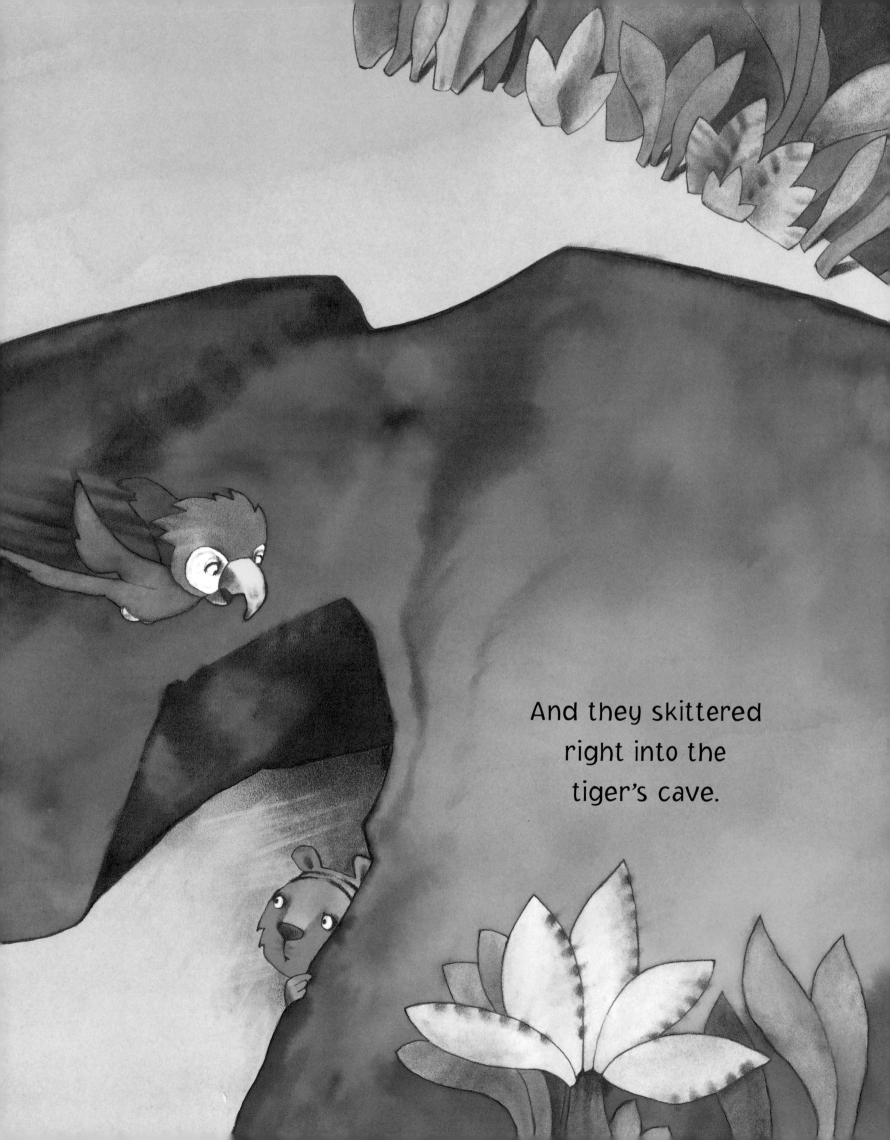

And they skittered
right into the
tiger's cave.

"You three should know
better," said Tiger. "There
aren't any dinosaurs in the jungle!"
"So you say!" cried Giraffe.

"But listen . . . listen!"

Then that tiger
heard the leaves
crunching. He saw the
mango trees shake.

"It's a . . .

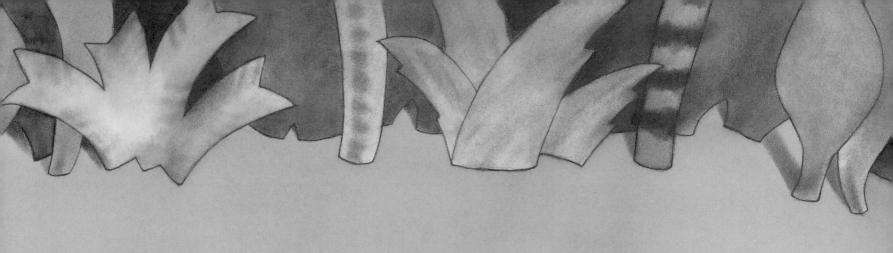

Dino in the jungle! Run away!"

And they skittered right
into the hippo's mud puddle.

"You four should know better," said Hippo. "There aren't any dinosaurs in the jungle!"

"So you say!" panted Tiger. "But listen . . . listen!"

Then that hippo heard the leaves crunching. He saw the mango trees shake.

"It's a . . .

Surprise!"

said Hippo. "I love a surprise! Let's see who is making all that ruckus."

Then those jittery animals stepped back while Hippo walked alone into the tall leaves.

Hippo stopped.

Hippo looked.

And Hippo turned
right around.
"That's no Dino,"
he said.

"That's a . . .

Rhino! There's a Rhino in the jungle!"

"Hello, Rhino!"